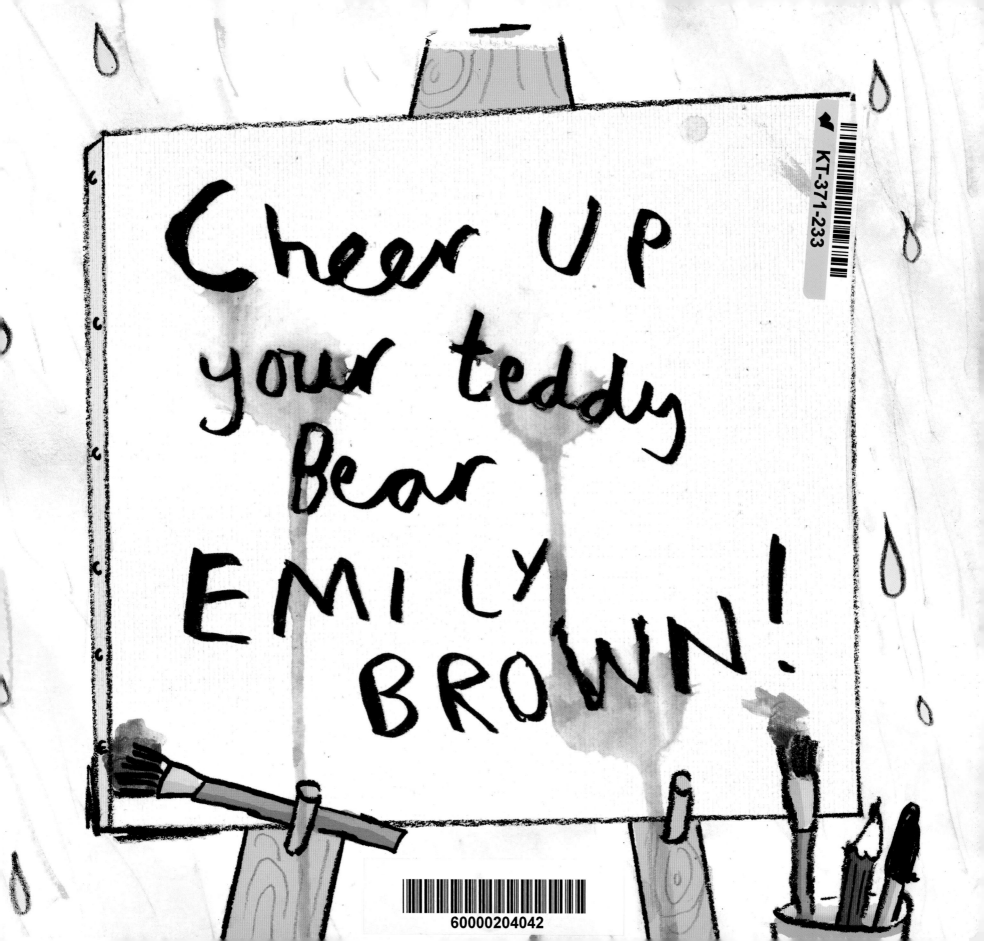

Cheer UP your teddy Bear EMILY BROWN!

For Sadie and Erica – N.L.

To Clemmie Cowell – C.C.

ORCHARD BOOKS
338 Euston Road, London NW1 3BH
Orchard Books Australia
Level 17/207 Kent Street, Sydney, NSW 2000

First published in 2011 by Orchard Books
First published in paperback in 2012

ISBN 978 1 4083 0849 3

Text © Cressida Cowell 2011
Illustrations © Neal Layton 2011

The rights of Cressida Cowell to be identified as the author
and of Neal Layton to be identified as the illustrator
of this work have been asserted by them in accordance
with the Copyright, Designs and Patents Act, 1988.

10 9 8 7 6 5 4 3 2 1

Printed in China

Orchard Books is a division of Hachette Children's Books,
an Hachette UK Company.

www.hachette.co.uk

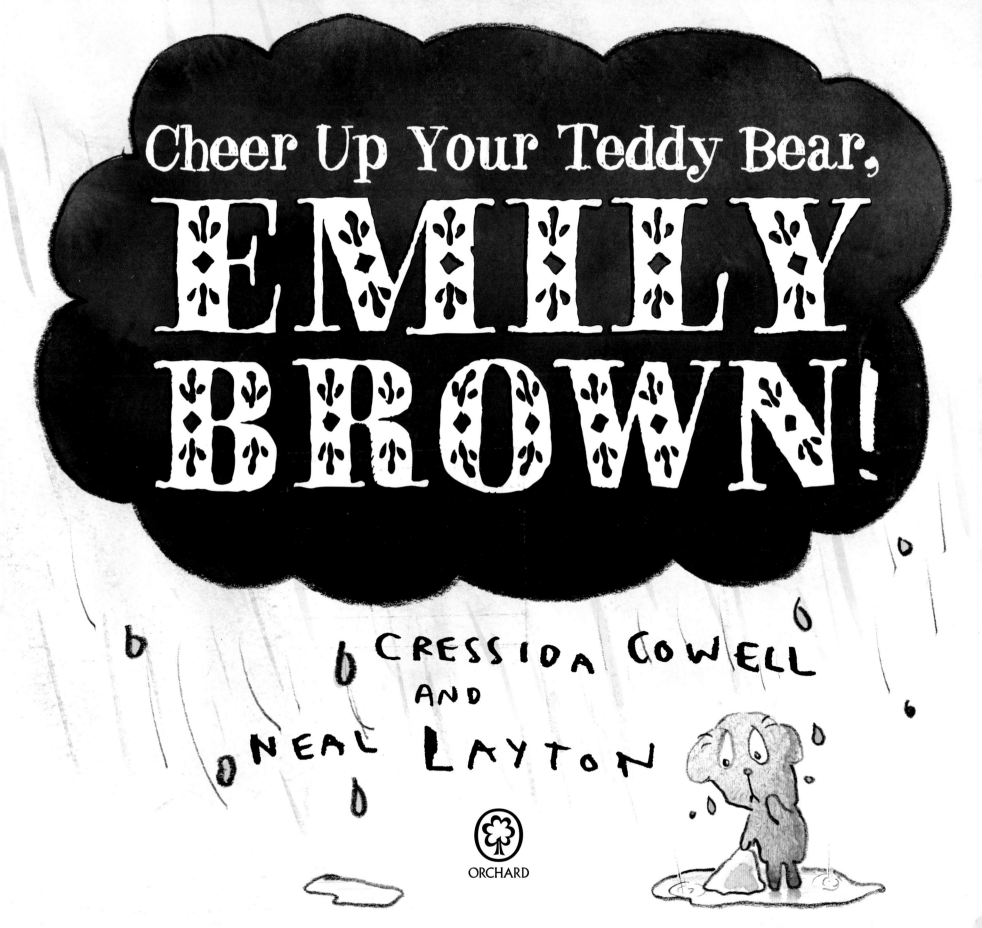

Once upon a time,
there was a little girl called Emily Brown
and an old grey rabbit called Stanley.

One drippy, drizzly, wet weekend, Emily Brown and Stanley were just building a camp in the Outback of Australia, because it was too rainy to go outdoors, when there was a **PLIP!PLOP!PLIP!PLOP!** noise coming from the toy-box.

'Uh-oh,' said Emily Brown to Stanley,
'I think there could be something wet in there . . .'
There certainly was.

It was a very wet teddy bear, and she was singing a song to herself
in a sad little voice, which went something like this:

'Po-o-o-o-o-or ME . . . po-o-o-o-o-oor ME . . .
Poor little sad little wet little ME . . .
I'm a Lonely Only Bear and I'm feeling very blue . . .'

'Come and have fun with us in Australia,' said Emily Brown.
'We're bound to find some bears there.'

'Thank you,' said the Tearful Teddybear, 'but there ARE no other teddybears.
I'm the lonely, only one.'

So Emily Brown and Stanley and the Tearful Teddybear
went out camping in the Outback of Australia.

And Emily Brown and Stanley were just as happy as could be, lighting campfires and spotting kangaroos and making friends with emus, and Emily Brown was just thinking, 'this will cheer up that Tearful Teddybear,' when there was a **PLIP!PLOP!PLIP!PLOP!** noise behind her . . .

. . . and it was the Tearful Teddybear, not cheered up at all.

PLIP PLOP! PLIP! PLOP!

'Po-o-o-o-o-or ME . . . po-o-o-o-o-oor ME . . .
Poor little sad little wet little ME . . .
I'm a Lonely Only Bear and I'm feeling very blue,
I've got no teddy friends and there's nothing here to do . . .'

'Oh dear,' said Emily Brown. 'Perhaps we should do something else.'

So Emily Brown and Stanley and the Tearful Teddybear
went out walking in the big wild woods of Yellowstone Park.

And Emily Brown and Stanley had a very happy time
spotting small bears and large bears and black bears and grizzly bears
but absolutely no teddy bears.

And Emily Brown was thinking, 'this is a lot of fun,'
when there was a **PLIP!PLOP!PLIP!PLOP!** noise . . .

PLIP!
PLOP!
PLIP!
PLOP!

. . . and it was the Tearful Teddybear, gloomier than ever.

'Po-o-o-o-o-r ME, po-o-o-o-o-o-o-o-o-o-or ME . . .
Poor little sad little wet little ME . . .
I'm a Lonely Only Bear and I'm feeling very blue,
I've got no teddy friends and there's nothing here to do,
I'm bored and it's raining and raining is no fun . . .'

'Oh dear,' said Emily Brown.

'Maybe we should try something different.'

So Emily Brown and Stanley and the Tearful Teddybear
packed their paintbrushes and their easels and their most arty looking overalls
and went to paint sunflowers in the south of France.

And Emily Brown and Stanley had the most lovely time splashing swirls of glorious blue and yellow and red all over themselves, and Emily Brown was just thinking, 'this is the funn-est thing ever,' when there was a **PLIP!PLOP!PLIP!PLOP!** noise behind her . . .

PLIP
PLOP
PLIP
PLOP!

. . . and it was the Tearful Teddybear, louder and sadder and more drippy than ever.

And this time, her song was so sad,

and so loud,

and so miserable

that a TERRIBLE thing happened.

Emily Brown and Stanley began to feel quite sad, too,
and then the clouds spread and spread until they filled the sky and
they got bigger and blacker and drip drip drip the rain came down
and it looked like it was going to wash away the sunflowers.

'This has gone far enough,' said Emily Brown.
She took out her red umbrella and pointed it up at the sky . . .

With a lovely swooshing noise UP UP UP UP UP went Emily Brown's beautiful red umbrella.

'Wow . . .' whispered Stanley.

UP! went Emily Brown's umbrella and, leaping out of the sunflowers, came one, two, three, four, five, six, seven, eight, nine, ten, eleven, **TWELVE** little teddy bears, who had been having a picnic, but were all in a hurry to get out of the rain!

'I'm not the lonely only Teddybear after all!' said the Tearful Teddybear.

'We've been here all the time,' the teeniest of the teddybears squeaked gruffly. 'And we'd really like you to join our picnic. But your song was so sad, we've been hiding.'

'I think,' said Emily Brown firmly, 'that it could be time for you to stop this sad song, and start smiling again.'

'Oh Emily Brown, Emily Brown,' wept the Tearful Teddybear.

'You see, that's the real problem.
Someone has sewn my mouth
on upside down, and I'm not
sure that I CAN smile…'

'Why don't you TRY?' said Emily Brown.
'Think of happy things, and see if that works.'

So the Tearful Teddybear screwed up her teddy forehead and tried to smile as hard as she could. She thought of all the other teddybears wanting to play with her and … **PING!** The left side of her mouth worked free of the stitches and waved happily in the wind.

And then she thought of the delicious picnic and . . . **PONG!**
The right side of her mouth unpicked itself and wriggled upwards
into a wibbly-wobbly smile. And a funny thing happened.

When the Tearful Teddybear smiled, the clouds got lighter and lighter, and the sun came out again and, as the very last raindrop dropped

PLOP!

onto the Cheerful Tearful Teddybear's head, all the little teddybears sat down for a picnic in the sunflowers.

But Emily Brown and Stanley went outside
to play in the rain . . .

. . . and they got very, VERY wet.